Toby

The American Tour of Messrs. Brown, Jones and Robinson

being the history of what they saw, & did in the United States, Canada and Cuba

Toby

The American Tour of Messrs. Brown, Jones and Robinson
being the history of what they saw, & did in the United States, Canada and Cuba

ISBN/EAN: 9783337382452

Printed in Europe, USA, Canada, Australia, Japan

Cover: Foto ©Andreas Hilbeck / pixelio.de

More available books at **www.hansebooks.com**

IN SETTLING THEMSELVES FOR THE VOYAGE, THEY ARE TROUBLED WITH CERTAIN QUALMS—WHICH ARE NOT QUALMS OF CONSCIENCE.

AFTER A PLEASANT PASSAGE, THEY SIGHT THE SHORE THEY SEEK. LAND HO! GENERAL TURN-OUT. ALL HANDS ON DECK. HAIL! COLUMBIA.

THEY RECEIVE THEIR FIRST INTRODUCTION TO THE CUSTOMS OF THE COUNTRY. THE MANNERS OF THE OFFICIALS, AND MODES OF EXAMINATION, STRIKE B., J., & R. AS BELONGING DECIDEDLY TO THE LAND OF THE FREE (AND EASY).

THEY ENCOUNTER THE BAGGAGE-SMASHERS, A NATIVE TRIBE (OF FOREIGNERS MOSTLY), NOTED FOR THEIR QUIET DEMEANOR, AND SUBMISSION TO AUTHORITY.

4

THEY DISCUSS A FINANCIAL QUESTION. A FARE DISPUTE WITH JEHU O'MULLIGAN, AN INFLUENTIAL CITIZEN. SOME KNOCK-DOWN ARGUMENTS ARE PRESENTED, BUT MR. O'M. KEEPS THE WHIP-HAND.

B., J. & R. "GO FOR" THEIR PICTURES, AND HAVE A "SITTING," STANDING. POSING, IMPOSING, AND UNIMPOSING. FRONT AND REAR VIEWS, WITH SIDE-ELEVATIONS.

SIGHT-SEEING—DINING.

TO SEE A PORTION OF THE CITY, THEY TAKE A COMFORTABLE RIDE ON A THIRD AVENUE CAR, AND FIND THEM-
SELVES STANDING ON A DEMOCRATIC PLATFORM WITH REPUBLICAN SURROUNDINGS.

THEY FIND OUR COLORED BRETHREN ENJOYING SOCIAL EQUALITY—AS MANIFESTED IN THE HOTEL DINING-ROOM.

6

BROWN FINDS A CHANCE TO STUDY A NATIONAL ATTITUDE, WHICH IS MUCH MORE COMMON THAN PROPER—A SORT OF TWO-FOOT RULE FOR MEASURING AMERICAN MANNERS. HE MAKES A SKETCH OF IT.

AT THE HIGH BRIDGE, THEY ENCOUNTER A HIGH WIND, WHICH TAKES LIBERTIES—THIS BEING A FREE COUNTRY— WITH ROBINSON'S HAT. THEY TURN THE ACCIDENT TO ACCOUNT, BY TIMING THE DESCENT OF THE HAT, TO ASCERTAIN THE HEIGHT OF THE BRIDGE.

AN UNPLEASANT NEIGHBORHOOD.

THEY VISIT A LOCALITY WHICH REMINDS THEM OF COLOGNE—NOT THE *EAU*, BUT THE CITY OF THAT NAME.

"A strange invisible perfume hits the sense."

AND, AS DISTINGUISHED STRANGERS, ARE ATTENDED BY A VOLUNTEER GUARD OF HONOR; WHICH TRIBUTE OF RESPECT THEY, WITH CHARACTERISTIC MODESTY, SEEK TO AVOID.

CENTRAL PARK.

B., J. & R. ARE RECEIVED AT CENTRAL PARK, WITH PRESSING ATTENTIONS BY THE CHARIOTEERS OF THAT REGION, WHO COURTEOUSLY TENDER THE USE OF THEIR VEHICLES.

BROWN SEES AND SEIZES (FOR HIS SKETCH-BOOK) A FAMILY LIKENESS. A POINT FOR DARWIN, BUT HARD ON JONES.

ANOTHER CENTRAL PARK SCENE, OFTEN SEEN AND BETTER UNSEEN.

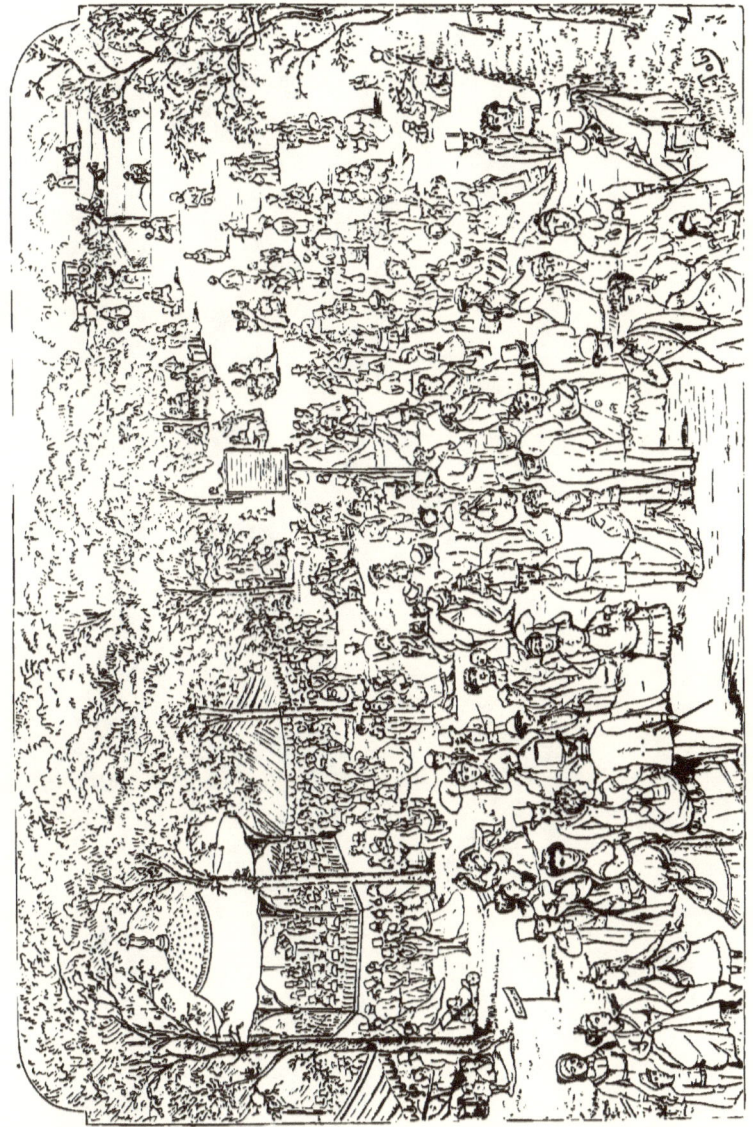

THEY VISIT THE MALL IN CENTRAL PARK ON A SATURDAY AFTERNOON, AND FIND VANITY FAIR IN FULL OPERATION.

IN THE GARDEN THEY ENJOY THEIR "WEEDS," AND ADMIRE THE FLOWERS—OF NEW YORK BEAUTY.

THEY ATTEND A REFRESHMENT CONCERT. MUSIC AND DRINKS—MIXED. ROBINSON, DESIRING TO TRY A NATIONAL DRINK, CALLS FOR AND CAUSES A "SMASH."

11

TRIP TO HOBOKEN.

B., J. & R., PURPOSING TO BOARD A STEAMER FOR HOBOKEN, HAVE A NARROW (BUT RAPIDLY WIDENING) ESCAPE, AND RECEIVE THE PANTOMIMIC CONGRATULATIONS OF A YOUNGSTER, NATIVE AND TO NO MANNERS BORN.

THEY VISIT THE ELYSIAN FIELDS, AND ADMIRE THE VIEW AND THE UNSOPHISTICATED MANNERS OF THE RURAL(?) POPULATION.

SKETCHES BY BROWN. TYPES OF HUMANITY (MOSTLY FROM FOREIGN FOUNDERIES) FOUND IN THE FIELDS.

NATIONAL GRATITUDE. MAIMED SOLDIERS PUBLICLY PROVIDED WITH—LEAVE TO EARN THEIR OWN LIVING.

SCENE ON THE GRASS. FREE AND EASY.

ANOTHER SCENE. FREER, IF NOT SO EASY.

CROSSING BROADWAY.

RETURNED TO THE CITY, B., J. & R. ATTEMPT A PASSAGE MORE PERILOUS THAN THAT OF THE ATLANTIC, TO WIT—CROSSING BROADWAY WHEN THE TIDE OF TRAVEL IS AT ITS HEIGHT.

SAFE OVER, BUT, LACKING THE COOLNESS OF THE NATIVE NEW-YORKER UNDER SIMILAR CIRCUMSTANCES, THEY ARE A LITTLE FLUSTERED.

14

UNIFORM COURTESY IN THE STREETS. ROBINSON TAKES AN OBSERVATION OF A POLICEMAN EMPLOYED AS AN INSTRUMENT OF TRANSIT. POLISHED POLICE POLITENESS.

JONES TRIES HIS LUCK IN ONE OF THOSE ADMIRABLE INSTITUTIONS, PECULIAR TO NEW YORK, WHERE BARGAINS ARE OFFERED AND CUSTOMERS "SOLD."—COMMONLY CALLED "MOCK-AUCTIONS."

REFRESHMENTS *AL FRESCO.* BROWN TAKES A SHINE FROM A NEW YORK BOY.

THEY VISIT THE BOARD OF BROKERS, WHERE "OUTSIDERS" ARE BROKEN, WHILE THE BROKERS REMAIN WHOLE.
B., J. & R. MAKE A "CALL" AND "PUT."

THEY VISIT CONEY ISLAND, AND "TAKE THE SURF" AS THE FANCY TAKES THEM.

THEY HAVE SOME "ROUGH" EXPERIENCE, AND LEARN HOW THE POLICE BACK THEIR VOTER FRIENDS

MORE OF BROWN'S SKETCHES. A CITY PORTER: BROWN, STOUT, AND "NEAT AS IMPORTED."

IN AN APPLE-VENDER BROWN FINDS A FRUITFUL THEME.

D., J. & R. START UP THE HUDSON RIVER IN ONE OF THE CONVEYANCES OF THE COUNTRY—"AH! NOT THE SORT OF THING WE HAVE ON THE TEMS, AND THE RHINE, YE KNOW."

JONES FINDS A FELLOW-PASSENGER, WHO, DESPITE THE WELL-KNOWN TACITURNITY OF THE YANKEE, IS QUITE READY TO INFORM HIM ON ALL POINTS OF IN- TEREST ON THE RIVER—AND WHAT HE DOES NOT KNOW, HE IS "GOOD AT GUESSIN'."

AND BROWN ENCOUNTERS A NATIVE BUT NEWLY- ENFRANCHISED CITIZEN, WHO DISCOURSES "OB DE FIF- TEENT' COMMANDMENT."

BROWN BESTOWS A GRATUITY WITH ULTERIOR VIEWS, TO WIT—THE HOPE OF REWARD BY A SYMPATHETIC GLANCE FROM BRIGHT EYES, PERHAPS.

THEY LAND AT WEST POINT. ROBINSON FORGOT TO LOCK THAT PORTMANTEAU, AND HERE'S THE CONSEQUENCE—
THE BAGGAGE-TRAIN THROWN INTO DISORDER AS THEY ARE ENTERING A MILITARY STATION.

REACHING COZZENS'S HOTEL, MR. COZZENS GIVES THEM A SPECIAL RECEPTION IN PERSON.

AFTER WHICH THEY APPEAR ON (SOCIAL) PARADE.

INVITED TO CADET PARADE, ROBINSON NATURALLY THINKS HIS YEOMANRY UNIFORM THE PROPER THING TO WEAR.

AND AT THE REVIEW HE ATTRACTS ATTENTION—AS HE MIGHT HAVE EXPECTED.

BUT IN RETURNING FROM CAMP HE FINDS HIMSELF UNPLEASANTLY MIXED UP WITH HIS OWN ACCOUTREMENTS.

THEY VISIT THE KAATSKILLS, AND, HAVING READ THE LEGEND OF RIP VAN WINKLE, BROWN DEVISES A COAT-OF-ARMS FOR THE LOCALITY.

IN ASCENDING THE MOUNTAIN, ROBINSON ACTS ON THE OLD ADAGE THAT "ONE GOES SAFEST IN THE MIDDLE;" AND TAKES HIS PLACE ACCORDINGLY.

THEY REACH THE MOUNTAIN HOUSE, A HOTEL IN *HIGH*
REPUTE; A LARGE INN WITH A WIDE OUTLOOK. THE HOUSE
IS NOTED ALSO FOR ITS FINE TABLE—OF SOLID ROCK.

AND THESE ARE THE EXPRESSIONS PRODUCED BY THEIR
IMPRESSIONS OF THE VIEW FROM THE MOUNTAIN.

WITH THE PROSPECT OF SOME CLIMBING-PRACTICE, THEIR ALPINE COSTUMES COME IN PLAY.

WHILE JONES DOES SOME "TALL" WALKING ROBINSON FINDS SOME CLIMBING A LITTLE TOO TALL—

AND THEREAFTER, HAVING FRIENDS, USES THEM. A HINT TO "HEAVY WEIGHTS" DESIRING TO RISE IN THE WORLD. WITH THE AID OF JONES AND BROWN, ROBINSON "PULLS THROUGH."

HAVING REACHED THE SUMMIT OF THEIR LONGINGS, B., J. & R. "FLATTEN OUT." AMBITIOUS ASPIRATIONS OFTEN END IN SMOKE—

ROBINSON TAKES A DIP.

OR ARE DAMPENED IN OTHER WAYS. WHILE EXPLORING "THE GLEN," ROBINSON MAKES A SLIP AND TAKES A DIP WHICH DOES NOT "ROCK HIM TO SLEEP." "SLIPPING UP" ON HIS "ALPINE STOCK," HE GOES IN FOR THE "POOL."

ACCEPTING THE SITUATION, HE FURNISHES A SUBJECT FOR THE DRY HUMOR OF BROWN'S PENCIL, WHILE REFLECTING ON THE MINOR MISERIES OF HUMAN LIFE.

AN ASTRONOMICAL TABLEAU.

RETURNING BY MOONLIGHT, THE PARTY FORM A NOVEL ASTRONOMICAL TABLEAU—*THREE* MEN IN THE MOON.

JONES, HAVING A FANCY FOR "PIGS AND CHICKENS," MAKES A SKETCH OF FARM-LIFE IN THIS COUNTRY.

ARRIVING AT ALBANY, IN A HEAVY RAIN, THEY HAIL THE ONLY COACH IN WAITING, AND STORM IT IN A BODY.

WHILE WAITING FOR THE SARATOGA TRAIN THEY LUNCH, AND MEET FOUL USAGE FROM FAIR HANDS. BROWN IS SERVED WITH A DISH IN A MODE NOT LAID DOWN IN THE BILL OF FARE.

CONGRESS WATER.

THE PIAZZA OF CONGRESS HALL, SARATOGA, WHERE IT IS QUITE IN ORDER FOR JONES TO HAVE A *TILT* ON INTER-NATIONAL POLITICS.

THEY VISIT THE CONGRESS SPRING, AND THE WATER PRODUCES ITS USUAL INSTANTANEOUS EFFECT ON A FIRST TRIAL—A SHARP DISTORTION OF FACIAL MUSCLES.

THEY WATCH THE MORNING ARRIVALS OF INVALIDS TO TAKE THE WATER.

THREE OF THE INVALIDS.   ANOTHER OF BROWN'S SKETCHES.

B., J. & R. ATTEND A "HOP" AT CONGRESS HALL, FINDING IT VERY MUCH LIKE A BALL ELSEWHERE.

AND BROWN, SLIGHTLY OVER-MATCHED, IS RATHER "CARRIED OFF HIS FEET" IN A LIVELY WALTZ *A DEUX-TEMPS;*

WHILE POOR ROBINSON MEETS WITH A *CONTRE TEMPS.*

THE BELLES OF SARATOGA—SOME OF THE "LOUDEST."

ON SARATOGA LAKE THEY HAVE A *QUIET* ROW BY MOONLIGHT.

GOING WEST, THEY TRY THE NOVELTY OF A SLEEPING-CAR, WHICH BROWN AND ROBINSON TAKE TO, BUT IN WHICH POOR JONES FINDS NEITHER REST NOR REFRESHMENT;

AND, ON ARRIVING AT UTICA, JONES IS RATHER DOWN.

AT TRENTON FALLS THEY HAVE AN ARITHMETICAL DIFFICULTY WITH THE LANDLORD, WHO OFFERS TWO BEDS FOR THE THREE—"THREE INTO TWO, YOU CAN'T."

ON STARTING TO SEE THE FALLS, THE GUIDES DISCUSS THE PROPER ROUTE TO TAKE.

JONES SETTLES THE DISPUTE;

AND THEY TAKE THE EASIEST PATH—WHICH STILL HAS ITS UPS AND DOWNS.

THE FALLS. TO GET A GOOD VIEW, THEY TAKE A BOLD STAND—NOT TO SAY A RASH ONE.

"GOING BACK ON" THE VIEW.

BROWN, THINKING HIMSELF ALONE, SEATS HIMSELF TO SKETCH;

AND FINDS HIMSELF NOT SO MUCH ALONE AS HE THOUGHT.

THEY TRY FOR TROUT. JONES DISGUSTED, BROWN DELIGHTED, WHILE ROBINSON HAS THE MOST QUIET ENJOY-MENT.

THEY ATTEND A PICNIC, WHICH WOULD HAVE BEEN VERY JOLLY BUT FOR NUMEROUS UNINVITED ATTENDANTS FROM VARIOUS INSECT TRIBES.

ON REACHING NIAGARA, B., J. & R. BECOME SLIGHTLY DEMONSTRATIVE.

THEY PURCHASE A FEW CURIOSITIES OF THE NEIGHBORHOOD—WHICH THEY MIGHT HAVE HAD AT LESS COST FROM THE MANUFACTORIES IN NEW ENGLAND.

BROWN SKETCHES THE FALLS FROM THE AMERICAN SIDE.

THEY ASCEND TERRAPIN TOWER, AND, FINDING IT IN A SHAKY CONDITION, ARE SYMPATHETICALLY AFFECTED.

TABLE ROCK.

IN TAKING A VIEW FROM TABLE ROCK, THEY DEEM IT PRUDENT TO TAKE A POSITION MORE SAFE THAN DIG-NIFIED.

IN PREPARING TO GO UNDER THE SHEET, THEY GET FITS. BROWN IS FITTED TOO MUCH.

IN THE CAVE OF THE WINDS, JONES'S NERVES GIVE OUT;

AND THE EFFECTS OF THE VISIT ON THE PARTY REQUIRE COUNTERACTING.

43

BROWN MAKES MORE SKETCHES—A "SO-CALLED" SPIRITUALIST;   A WOMAN'S-RIGHTS WOMAN;

A REPRESENTATIVE FENIAN;   AND A "LEADER OF PUBLIC OPINION."

B., J. & R. CROSS THE BORDER INTO CANADA, AND BEING AGAIN ON BRITISH SOIL, "YOU KNOW," ARE IN-
DIGNANT AT THE SEARCHING ATTENTIONS OF THE TORONTO CUSTOMS OFFICIALS.

THEY ARE ALLOWED TO PASS; BUT THE LAW, BY ITS AGENTS, KEEPS ITS EYE ON THEM.

THIS IS BROWN'S SKETCH (FROM MEMORY) OF THE MOST ATTENTIVE DETECTIVE WHO PERSONIFIED "THE OF THE LAW."

THEY COMPLAIN TO THE GOVERNOR, A GOOD FELLOW, WHO SOOTHES THEIR WOUNDED FEELINGS BY AN TATION TO A FOX-HUNT.

THE FOX-HUNT.

THEY ACCEPT, ARE MOUNTED ON INDIFFERENT, NOT TO SAY BAD, HUNTING STOCK;

AND JONES AND ROBINSON SOON COME TO GRIEF AND—GRASS.

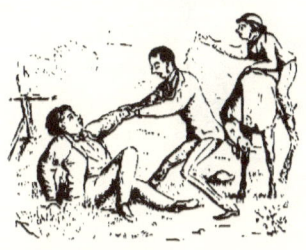

BROWN, MORE PRUDENT, KEEPS HIS SEAT, AND "ASSISTS" (IN THE FRENCH SENSE) AS THEY PICK THEMSELVES UP;

WITH NO MORE SERIOUS CONSEQUENCE THAN FINDING THEMSELVES "RACY OF THE SOIL,"

JONES, IN ASKING AFTER HIS LOST STEED, LEARNS THAT A CANADIAN *HABITAN* SPEAKS NEITHER FRENCH NOR ENGLISH, AND HE TRIES PANTOMIME TO AID HIS INQUIRIES.

ON THE RIVER ST. LAWRENCE, B., J. & R. HAVE EXPERIENCE OF A NOVEL SPORT KNOWN AS "SHOOTING THE RAPIDS;"

AND BROWN AGAIN SKETCHES—THIS BEING THE INDIAN PILOT—THE MAN WHOSE SPECIAL AIM IT IS TO DO THE SHOOTING ACCURATELY.

AMONG THE INDIANS.

THEY VISIT AN INDIAN CAMP WITH WHAT THEY CONSIDER THE PROPER *SPIRIT* OF CONCILIATION.

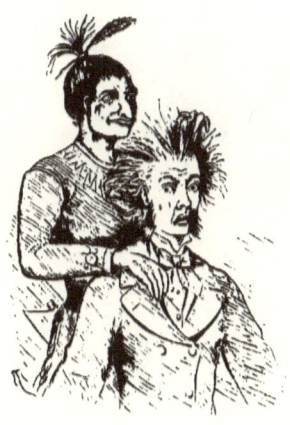

A FRIENDLY INDIAN, ATTRACTED BY THE "FAIR-HAIRED SAXON," CAUSES A LITTLE NERVOUS EXCITEMENT AS BROWN HAPPENS TO THINK OF SCALPS AND TOMAHAWKS; AND WHY SHOULDN'T HE!

CHOSEN MEMBERS OF THE TRIBE, THEY ARE COSTUMED ACCORDINGLY, ONLY JONES *CANNOT* FOREGO THAT UMBRELLA AND EYE-GLASS.

THEY TRY A SHOOTING-MATCH AT THE RAPIDS—IN THE ABORIGINAL STYLE.

THEIR COLLECTION OF INDIAN CURIOSITIES BRINGS UP THE QUESTION OF STOWAGE.

BROWN SKETCHES AGAIN—AN INDIAN GIRL;   AND AN INDIAN WOMAN.

AND AT MONTREAL HE FINDS A FRESH VARIETY OF CHARACTER-SKETCHES FOR HIS PORTFOLIO—THE ECCLESI-
ASTICAL ELEMENT BEING PREVALENT.

IN "DOING" MONTREAL CATHEDRAL DURING SERVICE, THEY EXCITE THE DISGUST OF HIS REVERENCE BY THEIR
IRREVERENCE.

BEING AT FUR HEADQUARTERS, SO TO SPEAK, OF COURSE IT IS THE THING TO FIT THEMSELVES OUT FOR THE SERPENTINE AND REGENT'S PARK AT HOME, THE COMING WINTER.

THEY RECEIVE AN ACCEPTABLE INVITATION TO AN AMATEUR PERFORMANCE AT THE THEATRE ROYAL;

AMATEUR THEATRICALS.

WHICH THEY ATTEND, AND—ARE AMUSED, TO SAY THE LEAST OF IT.

A SPECIMEN OF THE ECCLESIASTICAL ELEMENT SOLICITS CONTRIBUTIONS—FOR THE POPE'S ARMY, PERHAPS.

55

QUEBEC.

A STREET VIEW IN QUEBEC—B., J. & R. IN THE FORE-GROUND, WITH THEIR BACKS IN FRONT.

BROWN SKETCHES A TYPICAL CANADIAN ANNEXATIONIST AND CONSERVATIVE — LEAVING BUT LITTLE DOUBT
"WHICH OF THE TWO TO CHOOSE."

RETURNING TO THE STATES, B., J. & R. SEE THE BEAUTIES OF LAKE CHAMPLAIN UNDER ADVERSE CIRCUMSTANCES.

BROWN SKETCHES A VIEW OF ONE OF THEIR STOPPING-PLACES ON THE LAKE;

WHENCE THEY GO OUT TO TRY DUCK-SHOOTING;   AND RETURN—WITH QUALIFIED SUCCESS.

THEY REACH LAKE GEORGE RATHER LATE IN THE SEASON—

SO LATE THAT EVEN THE KITCHEN OFFICIALS "TAKE THINGS EASY."

FORT GEORGE.

ROBINSON TRIES HIS PENCIL ON A VIEW OF LAKE GEORGE. A SKETCH OF GREAT MERIT—THE MERIT OF GENERAL APPLICATION TO SO MANY INLAND WATER-VIEWS. EVERY TRAVELLER SHOULD LEARN TO DRAW IT.

AT THE RUINS OF FORT GEORGE—A REMINDER OF COLONIAL TIMES—JONES SENTIMENTALIZES, BROWN SKETCHES, AND ROBINSON MAKES HIS MARK.

BUNKER HILL.

ARRIVING AT BOSTON, BUNKER HILL MONUMENT—ANOTHER REMINDER OF COLONIAL TIMES—SENDS A SHAFT TO THEIR LOYAL HEARTS;

BUT THEY DO THE PROPER THING BY VISITING THE COMMON—

AND FIND THAT BROWN'S SKETCH OF THE "FROG-POND"—EVOLVED IN ADVANCE FROM HIS "INNER CONSCIOUS-NESS"—IS SLIGHTLY EXAGGERATED.

OF THE BIG ORGAN THEY ENDEAVOR TO GET A BOSTON ESTIMATE BY THE USE OF MAGNIFIERS OF PROPER POWER.

FOR THE HONOR OF THEIR COUNTRY, THEY ACCEPT A CHALLENGE TO A ROW ON THE CHARLES RIVER;

BUT ARE DISGUSTED TO FIND, AFTER THEIR EXERCISE, THAT LIQUID REFRESHMENT IS UNOBTAINABLE IN TEMPERATE BOSTON.

BACK IN NEW YORK IN DUE SEASON, THEY TREAT THEMSELVES TO A SLEIGH-RIDE IN CENTRAL PARK;

AND DISPLAY THEIR SKILL ON THE SKATING-RINK.

THEY ARE OFF TO CUBA, WHERE THEY ARE FIRST WELCOMED BY DON RAMON JIMENEZ VALDES DE ZORRILLA Y CONTO NAVARRO, OF WHOM BROWN GETS A SKETCH;

AND WHO POLITELY PRESENTS THEM WITH A PERMIT TO LAND, IN CONSIDERATION OF—ONE DOLLAR PER HEAD.

TAKING A *VOLANTE* AND *CALESERO* — THE INDIGENOUS COACH AND COACHMAN—THEY PROCEED TO THEIR HOTEL ;

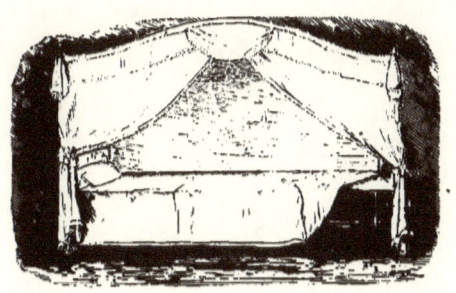

WHERE THEY FIND THAT A CUBAN BED IS ALL SHEETS AND CURTAINS, A MATTRESS NOT BEING DEEMED NECESSARY.

AT DINNER, ROBINSON LEARNS, FROM THE SIZE OF HIS CHOP, THAT MUTTON DOES NOT DEVELOP WELL IN A TROPICAL CLIMATE.

THEY EXPERIENCE A NIGHT ALARM. AN ATTACK ON BROWN'S CAMP (BEDSTEAD) BY SCORPIONS AND CENTI-PEDES. SOME OF THE BEAUTIES OF THE TROPICS.

IN MAKING AN EVENING CALL, B., J. & R. FIND THAT SMOKING IS A UNIVERSAL CUSTOM, WITHOUT REGARD TO "AGE, SEX, OR PREVIOUS CONDITION."

BROWN SKETCHES AGAIN — A NEGRO DANDY;

AND A STREET SCENE DURING A NEGRO FESTIVAL — A NEGRO DANCE IN FANCY COSTUME;

AND ONE OF THE MUSICAL INSTRUMENTS WHICH JONES PURCHASES.

BROWN'S SKETCH OF A CUBAN DANCE CALLED THE "MERENGUE."

A CUBAN BAND.

ONE OF THE INSTITUTIONS OF THE COUNTRY, WHICH WAS NOT UNKNOWN IN ENGLAND IN FORMER TIMES — A COCK-FIGHT.

BROWN ORDERS FIFTY CENTS' WORTH OF ORANGES. "WHAT WILL HE DO WITH THEM!"

GOING OUT TO SKETCH, THEY ARE TAKEN FOR SPIES BY THE CATALAN VOLUNTEERS, AND ATTRACT ATTENTIONS;

FROM WHICH THEY VOLUNTARILY RETREAT.

71

BROWN'S SKETCH OF THE NOTED HAVANA DWARF LOTTERY-TICKET VENDER—

WHO, IN THE CAFÉ "LA DOMINICA," INDUCES JONES TO INVEST FOR THE PARTY.

AND AFTERWARD OVERCOMES THEM BY ANNOUNCING
THAT THEY HAVE DRAWN THE HIGHEST PRIZE;

WHEREAT THEY ARE SO ELEVATED THAT ROBINSON
ELEVATES THE DWARF.

EMBARRAS DE RICHESSE. A REIMBURSEMENT OF ALL THEIR TRAVELLING EXPENSES, WITH "SOMETHING OVER."

PATRIA

AT HOME AGAIN!